Maggie's Coral Reef Adventure

by Kate Boehm Nyquist

illustrations by Kathleen McCord

MONTEREY BAY AQUARIUM®

886 CANNERY ROW, MONTEREY CALIFORNIA 93940

www.montereybayaquarium.org

The mission of the Monterey Bay Aquarium is to
inspire conservation of the world's oceans.

Text © 2001 Kate Boehm Nyquist
Illustrations © 2001 Kathleen McCord

Published in the United States by the
Monterey Bay Aquarium Foundation,
886 Cannery Row, Monterey, CA 93940-1085
www.montereybayaquarium.org

Printed on recycled paper in Hong Kong
by Global Interprint

Managing Editor: Michelle McKenzie
Project Editor: Miki G. Elizondo
Designer: Ann W. Douden
Editors: Susan Blake, Nora L. Deans

ISBN 1-878244-34-5

Dear Family,

You are about to take a trip with Maggie to explore
an underwater coral reef! As you travel along with Maggie,
you'll meet all kinds of animals and plants that live in the sea.
Some blend in or disappear and others pop right out at you.

All these sea creatures have one thing in common—
they all call the coral reef home. Whether under the sea
or on the land, homes are important to the creatures
who live there, no matter who they are!

You can learn more about coral reefs and
other ocean homes by visiting the
Monterey Bay Aquarium's web site at
www.montereybayaquarium.org

Enjoy and protect!
Kate Boehm Nyquist
and the Monterey Bay Aquarium

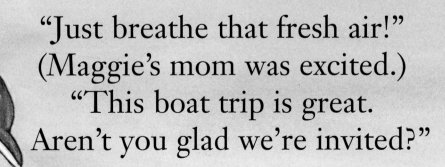

Maggie was bored
on the boat out at sea.
There was no one to play with—
No phone! No TV!

"Just breathe that fresh air!"
(Maggie's mom was excited.)
"This boat trip is great.
Aren't you glad we're invited?"

"There's nothing but waves."
(Maggie whined quite a lot.)
"The salt spray is sticky.
I'm seasick! I'm hot!"

"So let's dive," said her mom.
"The big reef's our next stop.
There's a lot more to see
underneath than on top."

"We get to go in?"
Maggie asked with delight.
That sounded like fun.
(Maybe mother was right!)

"You can snorkel," said mom,
"near the surface with me.
The reef isn't deep
but there's so much to see."

So they tied up the skiff
'til it held in the tide.
Then they put on their gear
and rolled over the side.

As the bubbles cleared off,
Maggie looked in surprise
as a beautiful world
opened up to her eyes.

The coral had shapes
that were both big and small.
There were some round and squat.
There were others quite tall.

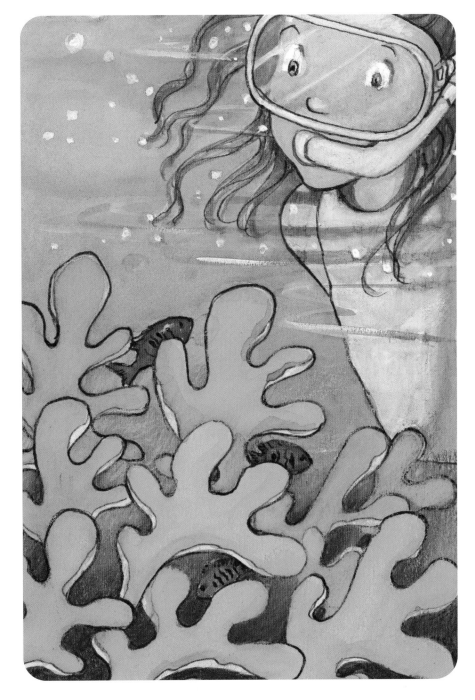

Green damselfish darted
all around, in and out;
while a butterflyfish
poked around with its snout.

A clownfish swam close
to a tentacle wall.
The anemone's sting
couldn't hurt it at all.

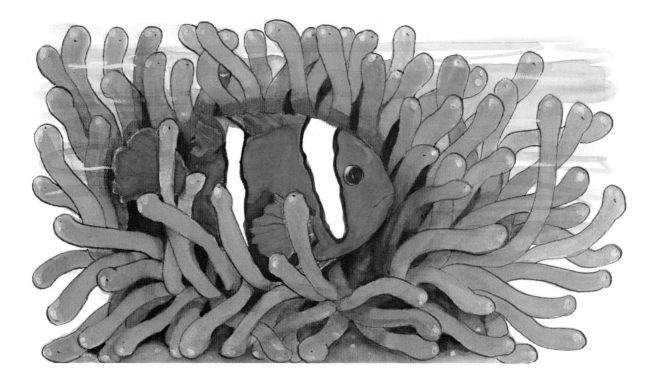

A hermit crab scuttled
across a sand track
to find a new shell
for a home on its back.

Sea stars and urchins
inched slowly along,
using suckers to move
with a grip that was strong.

Maggie's mom gave a sign.
In that hole! Something neat!
A huge moray eel
watched for prey it could eat.

Maggie startled a fish
—and its spines were a sight—
as a porcupinefish
puffed up big to give fright.

Maggie couldn't believe
all the life down below.
But her mom pointed "up"...
it was now time to go.

"So what did you think?"
asked her mom on the boat.
"Was I right? Was it fun?"
(She tried hard not to gloat.)

Maggie's smile was huge.
She just never had known
that so many live things
claimed the reef as their home.

"Well . . . it wasn't too bad."
(Maggie had to wisecrack.)

The truth was that she
couldn't wait to come back!